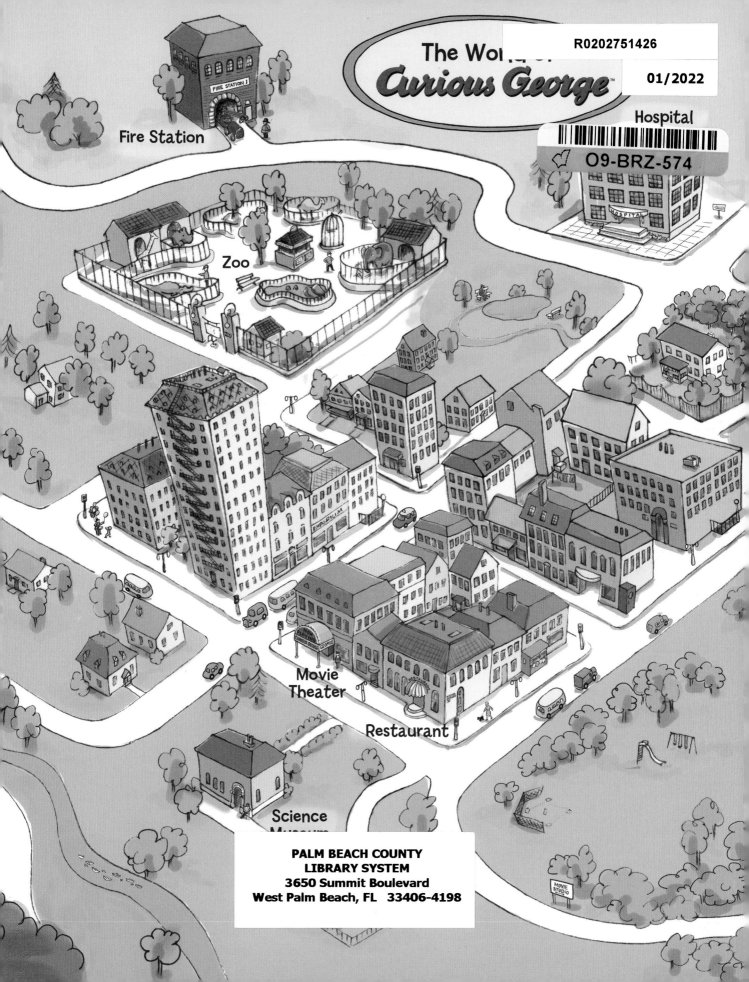

The World of
Curious George™

Fire Station

Hospital

Zoo

Movie
Theater

Restaurant

Science
Museum

THE COMPLETE ADVENTURES OF

Curious George®

75th Anniversary

75th Anniversary

THE
COMPLETE
ADVENTURES OF

Curious George®

MARGRET & H.A. REY

Houghton Mifflin Harcourt
Boston   New York

Contents

Curious George

by

H. A. Rey

Houghton Mifflin Company, Boston

This is George.

He lived in Africa.

He was a good little monkey
and always very curious.

One day George saw a man.

He had on a large yellow straw hat.

The man saw George too.

"What a nice little monkey," he thought.

"I would like to take him home with me."

He put his hat on the ground

and, of course, George was curious.

He came down from the tree

to look at the large yellow hat.

The hat had been on the man's head.

George thought it would be nice

to have it on his own head.

He picked it up and put it on.

The hat covered George's head.

He couldn't see.

The man picked him up quickly

and popped him into a bag.

George was caught.

The man with the big yellow hat
put George into a little boat,
and a sailor rowed them both
across the water to a big ship.
George was sad, but he was still
a little curious.

On the big ship, things began to happen.

The man took off the bag.

George sat on a little stool and the man said,

"George, I am going to take you to a big Zoo

in a big city. You will like it there.

Now run along and play,

but don't get into trouble."

George promised to be good.

But it is easy for little monkeys to forget.

On the deck he found some sea gulls.

He wondered how they could fly.

He was very curious.

Finally he HAD to try.

It looked easy. But —

oh, what happened!

First this —

and then this!

"WHERE IS GEORGE?"

The sailors looked and looked.

At last they saw him

struggling in the water,

and almost all tired out.

"Man overboard!" the sailors cried

as they threw him a lifebelt.

George caught it and held on.

At last he was safe on board.

After that George was more careful

to be a good monkey, until, at last,

the long trip was over.

George said good-bye to the kind sailors,

and he and the man with the yellow hat

walked off the ship on to the shore

and on into the city to the man's house.

After a good meal

and a good pipe

George felt very tired.

He crawled into bed
and fell asleep at once.

The next morning

the man telephoned the Zoo.

George watched him.

He was fascinated.

Then the man went away.

George was curious.

He wanted to telephone, too.

One, two, three, four, five, six, seven.

What fun!

DING-A-LING-A-LING!

GEORGE HAD TELEPHONED

THE FIRE STATION!

The firemen rushed to the telephone.

"Hello! Hello!" they said.

But there was no answer.

Then they looked for the signal

on the big map that showed

where the telephone call had come from.

They didn't know it was GEORGE.

They thought it was a real fire.

HURRY! HURRY! HURRY!

The firemen jumped on to the fire engines

and on to the hook-and-ladders.

Ding-dong-ding-dong.

Everyone out of the way!

Hurry! Hurry! Hurry!

The firemen rushed into the house.

They opened the door.

NO FIRE!

ONLY a naughty little monkey.

"Oh, catch him, catch him," they cried.

George tried to run away.

He almost did, but he got caught

in the telephone wire, and —

a thin fireman caught one arm

and a fat fireman caught the other.

"You fooled the fire department,"

they said. "We will have to shut you up

where you can't do any more harm."

They took him away

and shut him in a prison.

George wanted to get out.

He climbed up to the window

to try the bars.

Just then the watchman came in.

He got on the wooden bed to catch George.

But he was too big and heavy.

The bed tipped up,

the watchman fell over,

and, quick as lightning,

George ran out through the open door.

He hurried through the building

and out on to the roof. And then

he was lucky to be a monkey:

out he walked on to the telephone wires.

Quickly and quietly over the guard's head,

George walked away.

He was free!

Down in the street

outside the prison wall,

stood a balloon man.

A little girl bought a balloon

for her brother.

George watched.

He was curious again.

He felt he MUST have

a bright red balloon.

He reached over and

tried to help himself, but —

instead of one balloon,

the whole bunch broke loose.

In an instant

the wind whisked them all away

and, with them, went George,

holding tight with both hands.

Up, up he sailed, higher and higher.
The houses looked like toy houses
and the people like dolls.
George was frightened.
He held on very tight.

At first the wind blew in great gusts.

Then it quieted.

Finally it stopped blowing altogether.

George was very tired.

Down, down he went—bump,

on to the top of a traffic light.

Everyone was surprised.

The traffic got all mixed up.

George didn't know what to do,

and then he heard someone call,

"GEORGE!"

He looked down and saw his friend,

the man with the big yellow hat!

George was very happy.

The man was happy too.

George slid down the post

and the man with the big yellow hat

put him under his arm.

Then he paid the balloon man

for all the balloons.

And then George and the man

climbed into the car

and at last, away they went

to the ZOO!

What a nice place
for George to live!

H. A. REY

Curious George takes a Job

Houghton Mifflin Company Boston

This is George. He lived in the Zoo.

He was a good little monkey but he was very curious.

He wanted to find out what was going on outside the Zoo.

One day, when the keeper was not paying attention,
George got hold of the key for the cage.

When the keeper discovered what had happened, it was
too late—George was gone!

WHERE WAS GEORGE?

They looked for him everywhere.

But they could not find him.

George was hiding in the hay of his friend, the elephant.

Finally the keepers gave up looking for him.

George found a nice cozy spot to sleep under the elephant's right ear, and the next morning, before the Zoo opened, he got away safely.

Once in the street George felt a little scared. What should he do in the big city? Maybe he could find his friend, the man with the yellow hat, who had brought him over from Africa a long time ago. Only George did not know where he lived.

There was a bus stopping at the corner. George had never ridden on one. Quickly he climbed a lamp post, jumped on top of the bus and off they went.

Now they were right
of the town. There was
that George did not know
If only he could go on riding

in the center
so much to see
where to look first.
like this forever!

But after a while George got tired and a little dizzy.

When the bus slowed down to turn into a side street, George jumped off.

There was a restaurant right in front of him. Mmmm— something smelled good! Suddenly George felt very hungry.

The kitchen door stood open and George walked in.

On the table was a big pot. Of course George was curious.

He had to find out what was in it . . .

When the cook came back he had a big surprise. Spaghetti was all over the place and in the middle of it was a little monkey!

George had been eating yards and yards and had wound himself all up in it.

The cook was a kind man and did not scold much. But George had to clean up the kitchen and then do all the dishes. My, what a lot of them there were! The cook was watching George. "You are lucky to have four hands," he said. "You can do things twice as quickly.

"I have a friend who could use a handy little fellow like you to wash windows. If you would like to, I will take you over to him."

So they went down into the subway and took an uptown train to the cook's friend, who was an elevator man in a skyscraper.

"Sure I can use you, George!" the elevator man said. "I will give you what you need for the job. You can start right away. But remember—you are here for washing windows. Never mind what people inside the house are doing. Don't be curious or you'll get into trouble."

George promised to be good, but little monkeys sometimes forget . . .

George was ready to start. My, how many windows there were! But George got ahead quickly, since he worked with all four hands. He jumped from window to window just as he had once jumped from tree to tree in the African jungle.

For a while George stuck to his work and did not pay any attention to the people inside. Of course he was curious, but he remembered his promise.

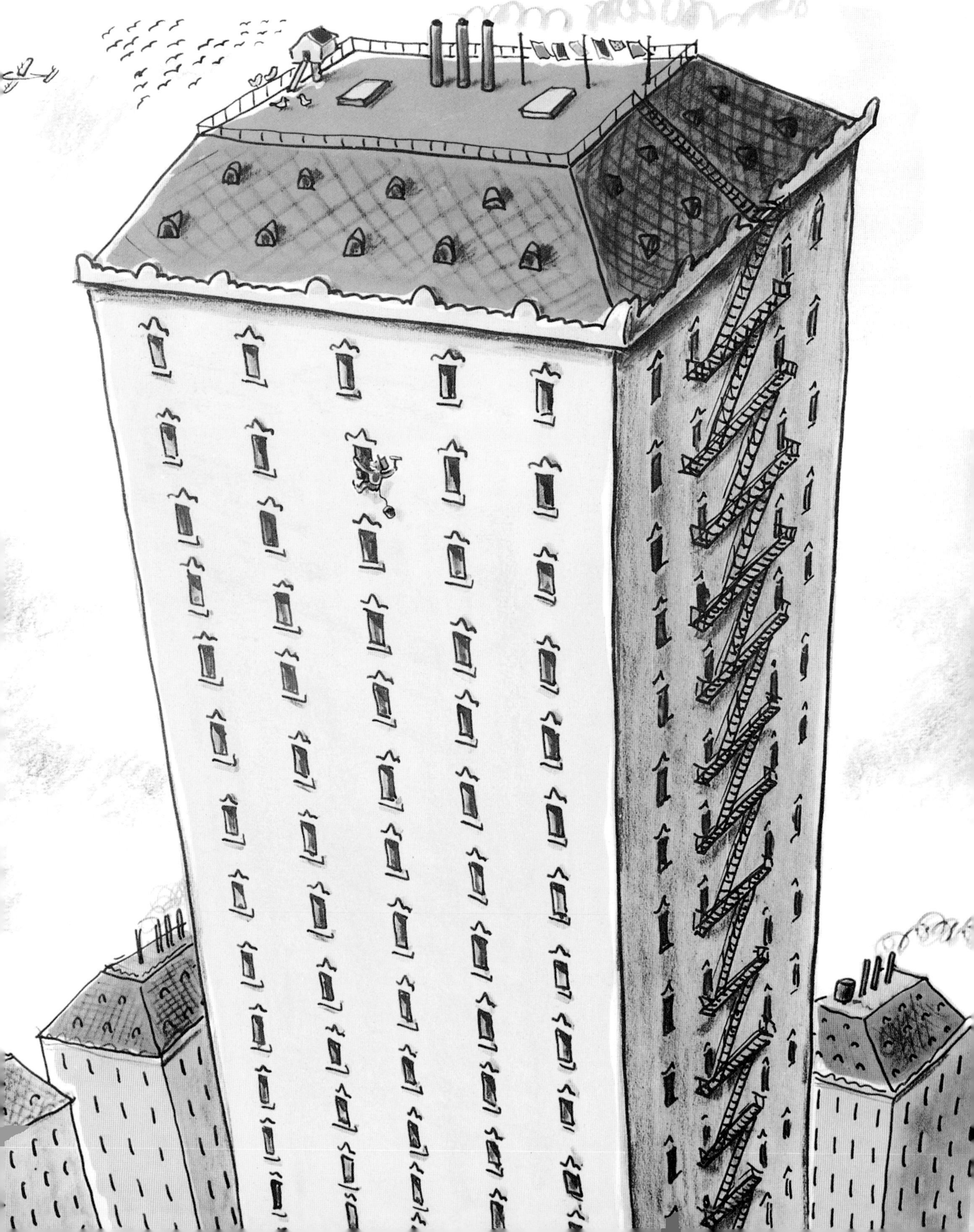

In one room a little boy was crying because he did not want to eat his spinach. George did not even look but went right on with his work.

In another room a man was taking a nap and snoring. George was sorry it was not his friend, the man with the yellow hat. He listened to the funny noise for a while, then went on working.

But what was going on in here? George stopped working and pressed his nose against the window. Two painters were working inside. George was fascinated. Painting looked like a lot more fun than washing windows!

The painters were getting ready to go out for lunch. The minute they left George climbed inside.

What wonderful paints and brushes they had! George

could not resist . . .

An hour later the painters came back. They opened the door—and stood there with their mouths wide open. The whole room had changed into a jungle with palm trees all over

the walls and a giraffe and two leopards and a zebra. And a
little monkey was busy painting himself on one of the trees!
Then the painters knew what had happened!

Luckily George was close to a door. He ran out as fast as
he could. After him ran the two painters, then the elevator man
and then the woman who lived in the place.

"Oh, my lovely room, my lovely room!" cried the woman.

"Don't let him get away!"

George headed for the fire escape.

George reached the end of the fire escape.

The others had not caught up with him yet.

Here was his chance. They could not jump!

But George could easily jump down and escape.

In a moment he would be safe!

Poor little George! He had forgotten that the pavement was hard as stone . . . not like the soft grass of the jungle.

Too bad! The fall broke his leg and an ambulance came to take George to the hospital.

"He got what he deserved!" said the woman. "Making my apartment into a jungle, indeed!"

"I told him he would get into trouble," the elevator man added. "He was too curious."

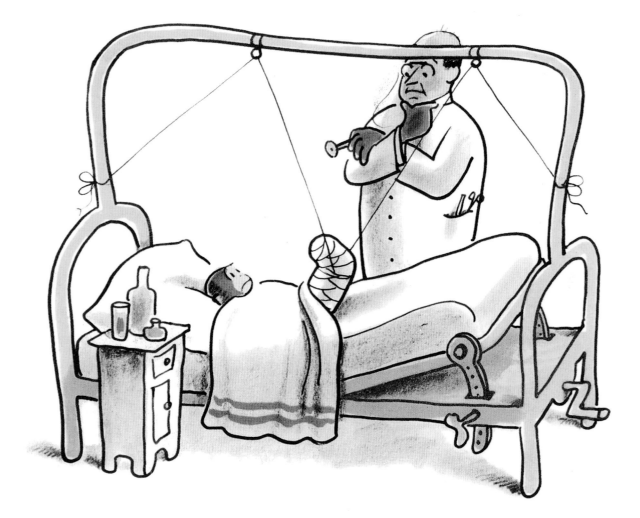

George had to lie in bed with his leg high up in a plaster cast. He was very unhappy.

And it had all started out so nicely! If only he had not been so curious he could have had a lot of fun. Now it was too late . . .

But next morning George's friend, the man with the big yellow hat, was buying his newspaper. Suddenly he got very excited. "This is George!" he shouted when he saw the picture on the front page. Quickly he read the whole story and then ran to a telephone booth to ring the hospital.

"I am George's friend," he said to the nurse who answered the telephone. "Please take good care of him so that he will get better quickly. I want to take him to a movie studio and make a picture about his life in the jungle. Don't let him get into any more mischief until I can take him away."

Finally the day came when George could walk again. "Your friend is going to take you away this morning," said the nurse. "Just wait right here for him and don't touch anything!"

As soon as George was alone he looked around at all the strange hospital things. "I wonder what is in that big blue bottle," he thought.

And this is how the man with
the yellow hat found George when he came to call for him!
They picked him up and shook him but they could not wake
him up. He was so fast asleep that finally they had to put him

UNDER THE SHOWER!

How surprised he was when he woke up!

George said goodbye to the nurse and the kind doctor.
Then he and the man with the yellow hat got into the car to
drive to the movie studio.

In the president's office George had to sign a contract.

Now he was a movie actor!

In the studio George was kept so busy all the time that he forgot to be curious. He liked the jungle they made for him and played happily there.

And when the picture was finally finished George invited all his friends to see it: the doctor and the nurse and the ambulance driver and the man from the newsstand and the woman and the elevator man and the two painters and the cook and the reporter and all the keepers of the Zoo.

Now the lights went out and the picture started.

"This is George," the voice began.

"He lived in the jungle.

He was a good little monkey—

he had only one fault: he was too curious."

H. A. REY

Curious George
rides a bike

Houghton Mifflin Company, Boston

This is George.

He lived with his friend, the man with the yellow hat.
He was a good little monkey and always very curious.

This morning George was curious the moment he woke
up because he knew it was a special day . . .

At breakfast George's friend said: "Today we are going to celebrate because just three years ago this day I brought you home with me from the jungle. So tonight I'll take you to the animal show. But first I have a surprise for you."

He took George out to the yard where a big box was standing. George was very curious.

Out of the box came a bicycle. George was delighted; that's what he had always wanted. He knew how to ride a bicycle but he had never had one of his own.

"I must go now," said the man, "but I'll be back in time for the show. Be careful with your new bike and keep close to the house while I am gone!"

George could ride very well. He could even do
all sorts of tricks (monkeys are good at that).

For instance he could ride this way,
with both hands off the handle bar,

and he could ride this way,

like a cowboy on a wild bronco,

and he could also ride backwards.

But after a while George got tired of doing tricks and

went out into the street. The newsboy was just passing by with his bag full of papers. "It's a fine bike you have there," he said to George. "How would you like to help me deliver the papers?"

He handed George the bag and told him to do one
side of the street first and
then turn back and
do the other side.

George was very
proud as he rode off
with his bag.

He started to
deliver the papers
on one side of the street
as he had been told.
When he came to the last house
he saw a little river in the distance.
George was curious: he wanted to know
what the river was like, so instead of turning back
to deliver the rest of the papers he just went on.

There was a lot to see at the river:

a man was fishing from the bridge,

a duck family was paddling downstream,

and two boys were playing with their boats.

George would have liked to stop and look at the boats,

but he was afraid the boys might find out that he had not

delivered all the papers. So he rode on.

While riding along George kept thinking of boats all the time. It would be such fun to have a boat — but how could he get one? He thought and thought — and then he had an idea.

He got off the bicycle, took a newspaper out of the bag and began to fold it.

First he folded down the corners, like this,

then he folded
both edges up,

brought the
ends together

and flattened
it sidewise.

Then he turned
one corner up,

then the
other one,

again brought
the ends together

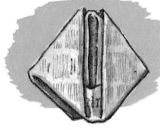

and flattened
it sidewise.

Then, gently, he pulled
the ends open —

and there was his BOAT!

Now the moment had come to launch the boat. Would it float? It did!

So George decided to make some more boats. Finally he had used up all the papers and had made so many boats that he could not count them — a whole fleet.

Watching his fleet

sailing down the river

George felt like an admiral.

But watching his fleet he forgot to watch where he was going —

suddenly there was a terrible jolt: the bicycle had hit a rock and George flew off the seat, head first.

Luckily George was not hurt, but the front wheel of the bicycle was all out of shape and the tire was blown out.

George tried to ride the bicycle, but of course it wouldn't go.

So he started carrying it, but it soon got too heavy.

George did not know WHAT to do: his new bike was

spoiled, the newspapers were gone. He wished he had listened to his friend and kept close to the house. Now he just stood there and cried . . .

Suddenly his face brightened. Why — he had forgotten that he could ride on one wheel! He tried it and it worked. He had hardly started out again when he saw something

he had never seen before: rolling toward him came an
enormous tractor with huge trailers behind it. Looking out

of the trailers were all sorts of animals. To George it looked like a Zoo on wheels. The tractor stopped and two

men jumped out. "Well, well," said one of the men, "a little monkey who can ride a bike bronco fashion! We can use you in our animal show tonight. I am the director of the show and this is Bob.

He can straighten your wheel and fix that flat in no time and then we'll take you along to the place where the show is going to be."

So the three of them got into the cab and drove off. "Maybe you could play a fanfare while you ride your bike in the show," the director said. "I have a bugle for you right here, and later on you'll get a green coat and a cap just like Bob's."

On the show grounds everybody was busy getting
things ready for the show. "I must do some work now," said
the director. "Meanwhile you may have a look around and

get acquainted with all the animals — but you must not feed them, especially the ostrich because he will eat anything and might get very sick afterwards."

George was curious: would the ostrich really eat anything? He wouldn't eat a bugle — or would he? George went a little closer to the cage — and before he knew it

the ostrich had snatched the bugle and tried to swallow it.
But a bugle is hard to swallow, even for an ostrich; it got
stuck in his throat. Funny
sounds came out of the bugle
as the ostrich was struggling with
it, all blue in the face.

Ogeorge was frightened.

Fortunately the men had heard the noise. They came rushing to the cage and got the bugle out of the ostrich's throat just in time.

The director was very angry with George. "We cannot use little monkeys who don't do as they are told," he said. "Of course you cannot take part in the show now. We will have to send you home."

George had to sit on a bench all by himself and nobody even looked at him. He was terribly sorry for what he had done but now it was too late. He had spoiled everything.

Meanwhile the ostrich, always hungry, had got hold of a string dangling near his cage. This happened to be the string which held the door to the cage of the baby bear. As the ostrich nibbled at it the door opened — and the baby bear got out.

He ran away as fast as
he could and made straight
for a high tree near the camp.
Nobody had seen it but
George — and George was not
supposed to leave his bench.
But this was an emergency,
so he jumped up, grabbed the bugle, and blew as loud as he

could. Then he rushed
to his bicycle.

The men had
heard the alarm
and thought at first
that George had
been naughty again.
But when they saw
the empty cage and
the ostrich nibbling
at the string, they knew
what had happened.

George raced toward the tree, far ahead of the men.

By now the bear had climbed quite high — and this was dangerous because little bears can climb up a tree easily but coming down is much harder;

they may fall and get hurt. The men were worried. They did not know how to get him down safely. But George had his plan:

with the bag over his shoulder he went up the tree as fast
as only a monkey can, and when he reached the baby bear

x

143

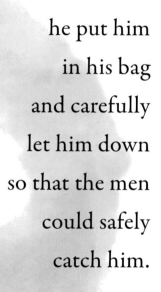

he put him
in his bag
and carefully
let him down
so that the men
could safely
catch him.

144

Everybody cheered when George had come down from the tree. "You are a brave little monkey," said the director, "you saved the baby bear's life. Now you'll get your coat back and of course you may ride your bike and play the bugle in the show."

Finally the show was on. The
and how surprised they were
right in the middle of it!
and also the man

whole town had come to see it,
to discover George on his bike
The newsboy was there, too,
with the yellow hat

who had been looking for George everywhere and was happy to have found him at last. The newsboy was glad to have his bag again, and the people from the other side of the street whose papers George had made into boats were not angry with him any more.

George!

When the time had come for George to say goodbye,
the director let him keep the coat and the cap and the bugle.
And then George and his friend got into the car and went . . .

good Night!

H. A. REY

Curious George

gets a medal

Houghton Mifflin Company, Boston

This is George.

He lived with his friend, the man with the yellow hat. He was a good little monkey — and always very curious.

George was alone this morning, looking at a picture book, when the doorbell rang.

It was the mailman.

"Here is a letter for you," he said. "Put it on your friend's desk. He'll read it to you when he comes home."

George was curious. It was not often that somebody wrote him.

Too bad he could not read the letter — but maybe he could write one himself! In the top drawer of the desk there was paper and ink and a fountain pen.

George sat down
on the floor and
began to write —
but the pen was dry.

It needed ink; George would have to fill it. He got a funnel
from the kitchen and started pouring ink . . .

But instead of going into the pen the ink spilled all over
and made a big blue puddle on the floor. It was an awful mess.

Quickly George got the blotter from the desk, but that was no help, the puddle grew bigger all the time. George had to think of something else. Why, soap and water, that's what you clean up with! From the kitchen shelf he got a big box of soap powder and poured all the powder over the ink.

Then he pulled the garden hose through the window,

opened the tap and sprayed water on the powder.

Bubbles began to form,
and then some lather,

and more lather

and more lather

AND MORE LATHER.

In no time the whole room was full of lather,

so full, indeed, that George had to escape in a hurry . . .

When he was safely out of the house he first turned off the tap. But what next? How could he get rid of all the lather before his friend came home?

George sat down in the grass and thought for a long time. Finally he had an idea: he would get the big shovel and shovel the lather out of the window!

But where WAS the lather? While George had been outside thinking, it had all turned into water. Now the room looked like a lake and the furniture like islands in it.

The shovel was no use — a pump was what George needed

to get the water out, and he knew just where to find one:
he had seen a portable pump at the farm down the road.

The farmer was away working in the fields. Nobody noticed George when he got the pump out of the shed.

It was heavy. He would need help to pull it all the way back to the house.

Maybe he could tie the goat
to the pump and make her pull it?
But just as George was about to slip
the loop over the goat's head —

he was hurled through the air
and landed near a pen full of pigs.

The biggest pig was standing near the gate. What if George opened the gate just enough to let him out? A big pig could easily pull a small pump.

Carefully George lifted the latch — and before he knew it,

ALL the pigs had burst out
of the pen, grunting and squealing
and trying to get away as fast as they could.
George was delighted. He had never seen anything like it.
For the moment all his troubles were forgotten . . .

But now the pigs were all gone and not a single one was left
to help him with the pump.

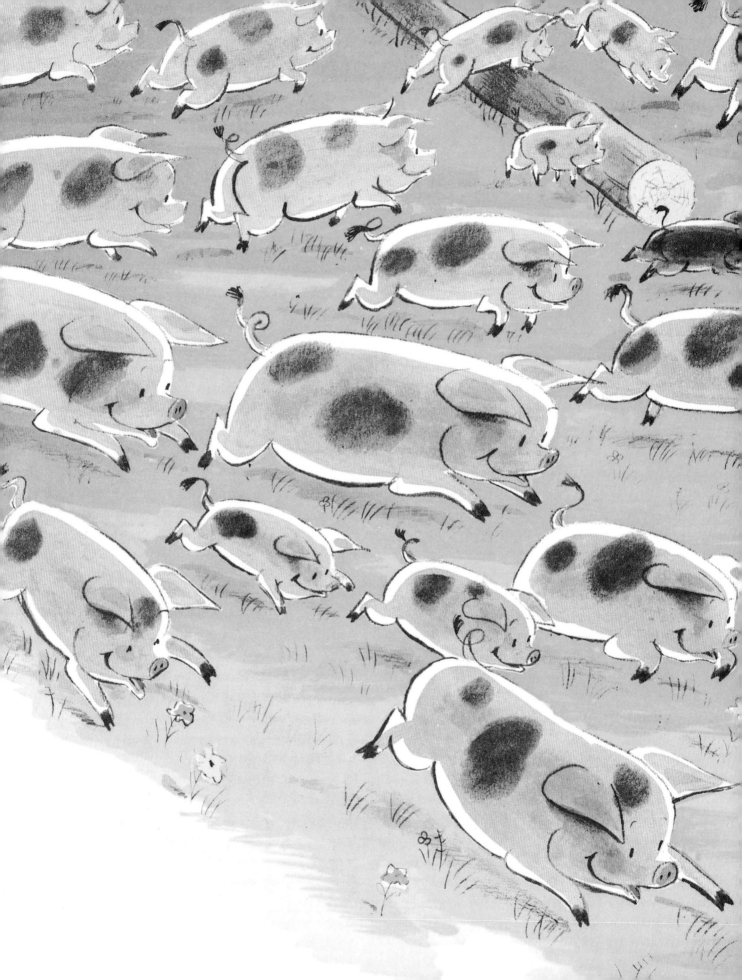

Luckily, there were cows grazing nearby. Cows were gentle and strong. It would mean nothing to a cow to pull the pump for him.

This time George was right, the cow did not mind being tied
to the pump. She even let him climb on her back — and off they
went! George was glad: now he would soon be home, pump out
the room, and everything would be all right.

Meanwhile the farmer and his son had heard the squealing of the pigs. They rushed home from the fields and now had their hands full catching all the pigs. Not until the last pig was safely

back in the pen did they have time to look around. And what did they see? A little monkey riding on their cow, making off with their pump!

The chase was on.
George and the cow
were ahead at first.
But the pump was
slowing them down.
The farmers were
getting closer and
closer.

Now they had almost caught
up with them — but
WHERE WAS GEORGE?

Here he was — hiding in a shirt! The farmers had run past him. But on their way home they had to come back over the same road. George did not feel safe in his hiding place . . . Just then a truck came rattling down the road.

George jumped aboard (monkeys
are good at jumping)
and was gone
before the farmers
had a chance
to see him.

MUSEUM OF SCIENCE

The truck drove to a part of town that George had never seen before. At last it stopped in front of a large building. It was the Museum. George did not know what a Museum was. He was curious. While the guard was busy reading his paper, George slipped inside.

He walked up the steps and into a room full of all sorts of animals. At first George was scared, but then he noticed that they did not move. They were not alive, they were stuffed animals, put into the Museum so that everybody could get a good look at them.

In the next room George saw something so enormous it took his breath away. It was a dinosaur. George was not scared this time; he knew it was not real. He looked at the dinosaur and then at the baby dinosaur — and then he saw the palm tree full of nuts.

Do not touch!

BABY DINOSAUR

George liked nuts. Suddenly he felt very hungry (he had missed
lunch that day). He would climb up and . . . Just then he heard
footsteps. He had to hide again — but where?

A family came in to take a look at the dinosaur. They paid no attention to the little monkey who was standing there. The monkey did not move. He stood so still they thought he was just another stuffed animal . . .

George was glad when they were gone! Now he could pick the nuts. He climbed up the dinosaur's neck and started to pull, but the nuts would not come off (George did not know they were not real either). He pulled harder and harder, the tree began to sway . . .

CRASH! Down came the tree on the dinosaur's head, down came the dinosaur, and down came George!

Guards came rushing in from all sides, and underneath the fallen dinosaur they found a little monkey! They pulled him out of there and brought him to Professor Wiseman who was the director

of the Museum. Professor Wiseman was terribly angry. "Lock that naughty monkey up right away," he said, "and take him back to the Zoo. He must have run away from there."

George was carried off in a cage. He felt so ashamed. Suddenly the door opened. "George!" somebody shouted. It was his friend, the man with the yellow hat! "It seems you got yourself into a lot of trouble today," he said.

"But maybe this letter here will get you out of it. It's from Professor Wiseman; he needs your help for an experiment. I found it on my desk at home — but I couldn't find YOU anywhere, so I came over here to talk to the Professor."

And this is what the letter said:

MUSEUM OF SCIENCE

Dear George,

A small space ship has been built by our experimental station. It is too small for a man but could carry a little monkey. Would you be willing to go up in it?

I have never met you but I hear that you are a bright little monkey who can do all sorts of things, and that is just what we need.

We want you to do something nobody has ever done before: bail out of a space ship in flight.

When we flash you a signal you will have to open the door and bail out with the help of emergency rockets.

We hope that you are willing and that your friend will permit you to go.

Gratefully yours
Professor Wiseman
Director of the Science Museum.

"So YOU are George!" Professor Wiseman said. "If I had only known . . . Of course everything will be forgiven, if you are willing to go."

They got the smallest size space suit for George and all the other things he needed for the flight. Then they helped him put them on and showed him how to use them. When everything was ready, a truck drove up with a special television screen mounted on it to watch the flight.

Check List

☑ 1 Space suit, complete with shoes & gloves

☑ 1 Space helmet

☑ 1 Oxygen tank

☑ 2 Emergency rockets

☑ 1 Parachute

They all got on and were off to the launching site. They checked all the controls of the space ship, especially the lever that opened the door. George tried it too.

The great moment had come. George waved goodbye and went aboard. The door was closed. Professor Wiseman began to count: "Five — four — three — two — one — GO!" He pressed the button and the ship rose into the air, slowly first,

and then faster and faster and higher and higher, until they could no longer see it in the sky. But on the screen they saw George clearly all the time.

Now the moment had come for George to bail out. Professor Wiseman flashed the signal. They watched the screen: George did not move. Why didn't he pull the lever? In a few seconds it would be too late. The ship would be lost in outer space with George in it!

They waited anxiously . . .
At last George began to move.
Slowly, as if in a daze,
he was groping for the lever.
Would he reach it in time?
There — he had grabbed it!
The door opened —
hurrah — George
was on his way!

    Out of the blue
an open parachute came floating down to earth. The truck raced
over to the spot where George would land.

What a welcome for George!

Professor Wiseman hung a big golden medal around his neck. "Because," he said, "you are the first living being to come back to earth from a space flight." And on the medal it said: To GEORGE, THE FIRST SPACE MONKEY.

Then a newspaperman took his picture and everybody shouted and cheered, even the farmer and his son, and the kind woman from next door (who had worked for hours to get the water out of the room).

"I'm proud of you, George," said the man with the
yellow hat. "I guess the whole world is proud of you today."
It was the happiest day in George's life.

The End

MARGRET REY

Curious George Flies a Kite

Pictures by
H. A. REY

This is George.

He lives in the house

of the man with the yellow hat.

George is a little monkey,

and all monkeys are curious.

But no monkey

is as curious as George.

That is why his name is

Curious George.

"I have to go out now,"
said the man with the yellow hat.
   "Be a good little monkey
till I come back.
   Have fun and play
with your new ball,
but do not be too curious."
   And the man went out.

It was
a lot of fun
for George
to play with
his big new ball.
    The ball
went up,
and George
went up,

and the ball
went down,
and George
went down.

George could
do a lot of tricks
with his ball too.
This was one
of the tricks.
He could get up
on the ball like this.

Or do it this way,
with his head down.

This was
another trick
George could do.
He could hold
the ball on his head,
like this.

Look—no hands.
What a good trick!
But—but where did the ball go?

George ran after it.

The ball had gone

into another room.

There was
a big window
in the room.

George liked to look
out of that window.

He could see
a lot from there.

He let the ball go
and looked out.

George
could see
Bill on his bike
and the lake
with a boat
on it.

George
could see
a big house
in a little garden
and a little house
in a big garden.

The big house
was the house
where Bill lived.

But who lived
in the little house?

George was curious.

Who could live in a house
that was so little?

George had to find out,

so he went to the big garden.

The garden had a high wall,

but not too high for a monkey.

George got up on the wall.

All he had to do now
was jump down—
so George jumped down
into the big garden.

Now he could take a good look
at the little house.

And what did he see?

A big white bunny
and a lot of little bunnies.

George looked and looked and looked.

Bunnies were something new to him.

How funny they were!

The big bunny

was Mother Bunny.

She was as big as George.

But the little bunnies were so little

that George could hold

one of them in his hand,

and that is what he wanted to do.

How could he get a bunny
out of the house?

A house must have a door
to get in and to get out.

But where was the door
to the bunny house?

Oh—there it was!

George put his hand in
and took out
a baby bunny.

What fun it was
to hold a baby bunny!
And the bunny did not mind.
It sat in his hand,
one ear up and one ear down
and looked at George,
and George looked back at it.

Now he and the bunny
could play in the garden.

They could play a game.

They could play Get the Bunny.

George would let the bunny hop away,
and then he would run after it
and get it back.

George put the bunny down.

Then he looked away.

One—two—run!

The bunny was off like a shot.

George did not look.

Now he had to wait a little.

One—two—three—four—he waited.

Then George looked up.

Where was the bunny?

He could not see it.

Where was it?

Where had it gone?

George looked for it here,
and he looked for it there.

He could not find it.

Where was the bunny?

It could not get
out of the garden.

It could not get up the wall
the way George could.

It could not fly away.

It had to be here—
but it was not.

The bunny was gone,
and all the fun
was gone too.

George sat down.

He had been a bad little monkey.

Why was he so curious?

Why did he let the bunny go?

Now he could not put it

back into the bunny house

where it could be

with Mother Bunny.

Bad monkey!

Mother Bunny—George looked up.

Why, that was it!

Mother Bunny could help him!

George got up.

He had to have some string.

Maybe there was some in the garden.

Yes, there was a string
and a good one too.

George took the string
and went back
to the bunny house.

Mother Bunny

was at the door.

George let her out

and put the string on her.

And Mother Bunny knew what to do.

Away she went
with her head down
and her ears up.
    All George could do was
hold the string
and run after her.

And then Mother Bunny sat down.

She saw something,

and George saw it too.

Something white

that looked like a tail,

like the tail of the baby bunny.

And that is what it was!

But where was the rest of the bunny?

It was down in a hole.

A bunny likes to dig a hole
and then go down and live in it.

But this bunny was too little
to live in a hole.

It should live in a bunny house.

So George got hold
of the little white tail
and pulled the baby bunny out.

Then they all ran back
to the bunny house.

George did not have to put a string
on the baby bunny.

It ran after its mother
all the way home.

George took the string
off Mother Bunny
and helped them back
into the house.

Then Mother Bunny,
and all the little ones
lay down to sleep.

George looked at them.

It was good to see the baby bunny
back where it should be.

And now George would go
back to where he should be.

When he came to the wall,
he could see something funny
in back of it.

George got up on the wall
to find out what it was.

He saw
a long string
on a long stick.
A fat man
had the long stick
in his hand.
What could the man do
with a stick that long?
George was curious.

The fat man was
on his way to the lake,
and soon George was
on his way to the lake too.

The man took a hook
out of his box,
put it on a string
and then put something on the hook.

234

Then the man let the string
down into the water
and waited.

Now George knew!

The string on the stick
was to fish with.

When the man pulled the string
out of the water,
there was a big fish on the hook.
George saw the man
pull one fish after another
out of the lake,
till he had
all the fish
he wanted.

What fun
it must be to fish!

George wanted to fish too.

He had his string.

All he needed was a stick,
and he knew where to get that.

George ran home as fast as he could.

In the kitchen
he took the mop
off the kitchen wall.
The mop would make
a good stick.
Now George had the string and the stick.
He was all set to fish.

Or was he?

Not yet.

George had to have a hook
and on the hook something
that fish like to eat.

Fish would like cake,
and George knew where to find some.

But where could he get a hook?

Why—there was a hook
for the mop on the kitchen wall!

It would have
to come out.

With the hook

on the string

and the string

on the stick

and the cake

in the box

in his hand,

George went back

to the lake.

George sat down,

put some cake on the hook,

and let the line down into the water.

Now he had to wait,

just as the man had waited.

George was curious.

The fish were curious too.

All kinds of fish came
to look at the line,
big fish and little fish,
fat fish and thin fish,
red fish and yellow fish
and blue fish.

One of them was near the hook.

The cake was just what he wanted.

George sat and waited.

Then the line shook.

There must be a fish on the hook.

George pulled the line up.

The cake was gone,

but no fish was on the hook.

Too bad!

George put more cake on the hook.

Maybe this time

he would get a fish.

But no!

The fish just took the cake

off the hook

and went away.

Well, if George

could not get the fish,

the fish would not get the cake.

George would eat it.

He liked cake too.

He would find another way

to get a fish.

George looked into the water.
That big red one there
with the long tail!
It was so near,
maybe he could get it
with his hands.

George got down

as low as he could,

and put out his hand.

SPLASH!

Into the lake he went!

The water was cold and wet
and George was cold and wet too.

This was no fun at all.

When he came out of the water,

Bill was there with his kite.

"My, you are wet!" Bill said.

"I saw you fall in,

so I came to help you get out.

Too bad you did not get a fish!

But it is good the fish

did not get you."

"Now I can show you how high
my kite can fly," Bill went on.
Bill put his bike up near a tree
and then they ran off.

There was a lot of wind that day,

and that was just what they needed.

The wind took the kite up fast.

George was too little

to hold it in this wind.

A kite that big
could fly away with him.
So Bill had to hold it.
George saw the kite
go up and up and up.
What fun it was to fly a kite!

They let the kite fly

for a long time

till Bill said,

"I will get the kite down now.

I must go home

and you should too."

But when Bill pulled the string in,

the kite got into the top

of a high tree.

Bill could not get it down.

"Oh, my fine new kite!
I can not let go of it.
I must have it back,"
Bill said.
"But the tree
is too high for me."

But no tree
was too high for George.
He went up to the top
in no time.

Then, little by little,

he got the string

out of the tree.

Down he came
with the kite
and gave it back
to Bill.

"Thank you, George, thanks a lot,"
Bill said. "I am so happy
to have the kite back.

Now you may have
a ride home on my bike.

I will run back to the lake
and get it.

You wait here for me
with the kite,
but do not let it fly away."

George looked at the kite.

Then he took the string in his hand.

He knew he could not fly the kite

in this wind,

but maybe he could let it

go up just a little bit.

George was curious.

He let the string go a little,

and then a little more,

and then a little more,

and then a little more.

When Bill came back,

there was no kite

and there was no George.

"George!" he called.

"Where are you?"

Then he looked up.

There they were,

way up in the sky!

Bill had to get help fast.

He would go to the man

with the yellow hat.

The man would know

what to do.

"George is not here,"
said the man with the yellow hat
when Bill came.
"Have you seen him?"
"George and my kite
are up in the sky
near the lake," Bill shouted.
"I came to . . ."

But the man did not wait

to hear any more.

He ran to his car and jumped in.

"I will get him back," he said.

"I must get George back."

All this time

the wind took the kite up

and George with it.

It was fun

to fly about in the sky.

But when George looked down,

the fun was gone.

He was up so high

that all the big houses

looked as little as bunny houses.

George did not like it a bit.

He wanted to get down, but how?

Not even a monkey

can jump from the sky.

George was scared.

What if he never got back?

Maybe he would fly

on and on and on.

Oh, he would never, never

be so curious again,

if just this one time

he could find a way to get home.

Hummmmm—hummmmm.

What was that?

George could hear something,
and then he saw something
fly in the sky just like a kite.

It was a helicopter,

and in the helicopter,

hurrah,

was the man with the yellow hat!

Down from

the helicopter

came a long line.

George got hold of it,

and the man with the yellow hat

pulled him up.

George held on to the kite,

for he had to give it back to Bill.

"I am so happy

to have you back, George,"

said the man with the yellow hat.

"I was scared,

and you must have been scared too.

I know you will not want

to fly a kite again

for a long, long time.

You must give it back to Bill

when we get home."

"Hurrah!" Bill shouted
when George came
to give him the kite.
"George is back,
and my kite is back too!"

And then Bill
took George by the hand
and went with him
into the little garden,

and from the little garden

into the big garden,

where the bunny house was.

"Here is one of my baby bunnies,"
Bill said.

"Take it, it is for you!"

A baby bunny for George!

George took it in his hands

and held it way up.

It was HIS bunny now.

He could take it home with him.

And that is

what he

did.

H. A. REY

Curious George

Learns the Alphabet

This is George.

He lived with his friend, the man with the yellow hat. He was a good little monkey, but he was always curious.

This morning George was looking at some of his friend's books. They were full of little black marks and dots and lines, and George was curious: what could one do with them?

The man with the yellow hat came just in time.

"You don't tear a book apart to find out what's in it," he said. "You READ it, George. Books are full of stories. Stories are made of words, and words are made of letters. If you want to read a story you first have to know the letters of the alphabet. Let me show you."

The man took a big pad and began to draw.
George was curious.

"This is an A," the man said. "The A is the first
letter of the alphabet."

A

Now we add four feet and a long tail—
and the A becomes an ALLIGATOR
with his mouth wide open.
The word ALLIGATOR starts with an A.
This is a big A. There is also a small a.
All letters come in big and in small.

This is a small **a**

It looks like a piece of an apple.

George knew alligators and apples.
You could eat apples. Alligators could
eat you if you didn't watch out.

This is a big **B**

The big B looks like a BIRD if we put feet on it and
a tail and a BILL. The word BIRD begins with a B.
BIRDS come in all colors. This BIRD is BLUE.
George loved to watch the BIRDS.

This is a small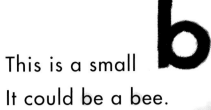
It could be a bee.

This bee is busy buzzing around a blossom.
The bee's body has black and yellow stripes.
George kept away from bees.
They might sting, and that would be bad.

This is a big

We will make it into a CRAB—
a big CRAB,
with a shell, and feet, and two CLAWS.

This is a small **C**

The small c is like the big C, only smaller,

so it becomes a small crab. It's cute.

Crabs live in the ocean.

They can swim or run sidewise and backwards.

Crabs can be funny, but they can also pinch you.

"You now have three
letters, George," the man said,
"A and B and C. With these three letters
you can make a WORD, the first word

you can read yourself. The word is

C A B

c a b

You know what a cab is. I once took you for a ride in a cab, remember? And now let's draw the next letter."

The big **D** could be a DINOSAUR.

There are no live DINOSAURS TODAY,
they have DIED out.
Those you see in museums are DUMMIES.
George had seen DINOSAURS in a museum once.

The small **d**
looks like a dromedary.

A **d**rome**d**ary is a camel with one hump.
Ri**d**ing on a **d**rome**d**ary can make you **d**izzy because
it goes up an**d** **d**own—up an**d** **d**own—up an**d** **d**own.

desert

The big **E**

is an ELEPHANT.
He is eating his EVENING meal: EGGPLANTS.
George loved ELEPHANTS.

The small **e**

could be the ear of a man,

or the ear of a monkey.
People's ears and monkeys' ears
look very much alike.

The big **F**

is a FIREMAN FIGHTING a FIRE.
Never FOOL the FIRE DEPARTMENT,
or you go to jail, and that's no FUN.

The small **f**

is a flower.
George's friend was fond of flowers.
George preferred food.

The big **G**

is a GOOSE.

GOOSE starts with a G, like GEORGE.

The small **g**

is a goldfish.
He is in a glass bowl and looks giddy.

"Now you know seven letters, George," said the man, "A, B, C, D, E, F, G. With these letters we can already make quite a few words. I have written some of them down: you read them while I get you your lunch."

"It seems the only word you can read is BAD," said the man when he came back. "I think we had enough for one morning. I'll feed you now and then you take your nap. After your nap we'll go on with our letters."

The big **H**

is a HOUSE.
It stands on a HILL behind a HEDGE.
George's HOME used to be a jungle.
Now he lives in a HOUSE.

The small **h**

is a horse.

He is happy because he has heaps of hay.

George had his own horse—a hobby horse.

The big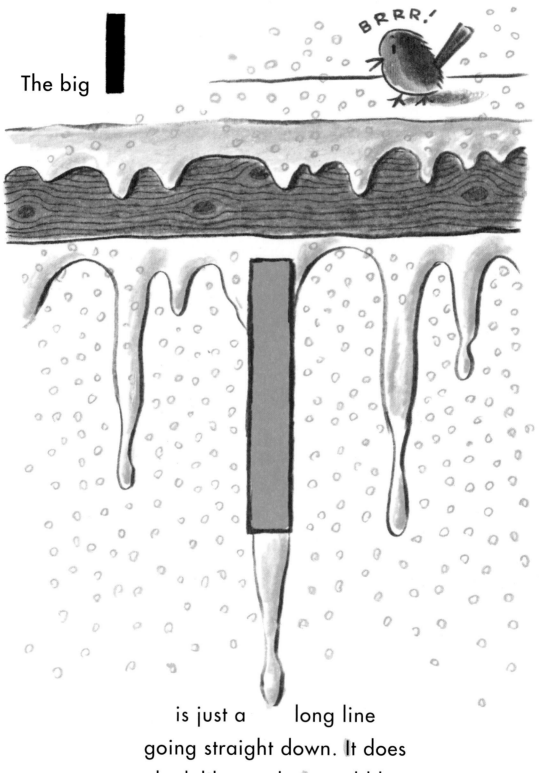

is just a   long line
going straight down. It does
not look like much. It could be an
ICICLE.

The small **i** is a line with a dot on top.
It could be an iguana.

An iguana is a sort of lizard.
Iguanas don't like ice. They like the warm
sunshine. So does George.

307

The big **J**
is a JAGUAR.

JAGUARS live in the JUNGLE.
George knew JAGUARS.
He had lived in the JUNGLE once.

The small **j**

is a jack-in-the-box.
George had a jack-in-the-box as a toy.
He just loved to make it jump.

The big **K**

is a big KANGAROO called KATY.

The small **k**

is a small kangaroo.
He is Katy's kid.

The big **L**

is a LION.
He is LUCKY. He is going to have
LEG of LAMB for LUNCH, and he LOVES it.

The small

is a lean lady.
She is strolling along a lake licking a lollipop.
George liked lollipops.

The big **M**

is a MAILMAN.
His name is MISTER MILLER. He brings a letter.
Maybe it's for ME, thinks George.

The small **m**

is a mouse.
He is munching mints.

"And do you know what else it is?" said
the man to George: "M is the thirteenth letter
of the A B C. The whole alphabet has only

26 letters, so thirteen is just half of it. You can make lots of words with these letters. Why don't you try? Here's a pad and pencil."

George started to think of words, and then he wrote them down. It was fun to make words out of letters.

"Let me see," said the man. "Ball–Milk–
Cake–Ham–Jam–Egg–Lime–Feed–Kid–
that's very good.

But what on earth is a Dalg or a Glidj or
a Blimlimlim? There are no such things. Just
ANY letters do not make words, George.

Well, let's look at some new letters now."

The big **N**

is a NAPKIN
standing on a dinner plate. It looks NEAT.
George had seen NAPKINS folded that way
in the restaurant when he was a dishwasher.

The small

is a nose
in the face of a man.
He has a new blue necktie on
and is nibbling noodles.

The big

is a big OSTRICH,

and the small  O

is a small ostrich, of course.

Ostriches eat odd objects.
One ostrich once had tried to eat a bugle that
belonged to George.

The big **P**

is a big PENGUIN,

and the small  is a small penguin.

These penguins live near the South Pole.
They use their flappers as paddles.
George knew penguins from the Zoo.

PLOP!

The big **Q**

is a QUAIL.
QUAILS have short tails.
You must keep QUIET if you want to
watch QUAILS. They are quite shy.

The small **q** is a quarterback.

A quarterback has to be quick. George was quick. He would qualify for quarterback.

"And now get your football, George," said the man, "it will do you good to play a little before we go on with your letters."

George knew how to play the game. He knew how to carry the ball,

and how to take a three-point stance,

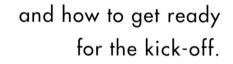

and how to get ready for the kick-off.

He was a fine halfback, too,

and he could make a short pass,
or recover a fumble.

"Good game," said the man, "but
time's up now: back to the alphabet!"

The big **R**

is a RABBIT.

Some RABBITS are white with RED eyes.

RABBITS love RADISHES.

George loved RABBITS. He had one as a pet.

The small **r**

is a rooster.

The rooster crows when the sun rises.

Two roosters will start a rumpus.

They really can get rough.

The big **S**

is a big SNAIL,

and the small  **S**

is a small snail.
Snails are slow. They sneak into their shells
when they are scared of something.
George thought snails looked silly.

The big **T**

is a TABLE.

The TABLE is set for TWO. It is TIME for TEA.

George did not care for TEA,

but he liked TOAST.

The small  is a tomahawk.

George had a toy tomahawk.
It was a tiny one.
He took it along when he played outside.

"Now it's time for a snack," said the man. "Run over to the baker, George,

and hand him this note. Then come right back with the doughnuts, one dozen of them, and no tricks, please!"

George was curious. He looked at the note the man had written. One dozen doughnuts . . . Maybe he could write something on it too? How about writing TEN instead of ONE? He had just learned the T . . . First a T — then an E — then an N . . .

"Hmm," said the baker,
"ten dozen doughnuts is
quite a lot, but that's
what the note says.
We need an extra-big
bag for them."

"Why, George!" cried the man.
Then he saw the note.
"Well, that comes from teaching
the alphabet to a little monkey.
And I told you: no tricks!"

"You may not eat any
doughnuts now, George.
Put them back in the bag
and let's go on with
the letters!"

U

The big **U** is a big UMBRELLA standing UPRIGHT.

The umbrella handle is also like a **u**.

George knew how to USE an UMBRELLA.

The small **U**
is a small umbrella.

When it is raining umbrellas are useful
but you must keep under the umbrella
unless you want to get wet.
George thought rain was a nuisance.

The big **V**

is a big VALENTINE,

and the small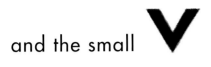

is a small valentine.
George loved valentines.
He got several valentine cards every year.
One card came from Nevada.

The big **W** and the small **W**
are WHISKERS, big ones and small ones.

A WALRUS has WHISKERS.

Some men  have whiskers.

and cats have whiskers.

George did not have whiskers
but he was curious how
he would look if he did.

The next letter of the alphabet is X.

The big  and the small **x**
look alike, only one is big and one is
small, just like the big W and the small w,
or the V, or the U, or the S, and some of
the other letters.

"But," said the  man, "there are
few words that start with an
X, and they don't look like an X—

except one, and that is
Xmas!"

Santa stands for Xmas.
There is only one Santa so we need only one
picture. George thought Xmas was exciting.

The big **Y**

is a big YAK

and the small **y**

is a small yak: he is still young.
Yaks live in Tibet. If you haven't seen any yaks yet
you may find one at the zoo.

The big **Z**

is a big ZEBRA,

and the small **Z** is a small zebra.

The zebras are zipping along with zest.

"And do you know what?" said the man, "Z is the last letter. Now you know all the 26 letters of the alphabet—

and NOW you may have the doughnuts."

Curious George

Goes to the Hospital

by

Margret & H. A. Rey

This is George.

He lived with his friend, the man with the yellow hat. He was a good little monkey, but he was always curious.

Today George was curious about the big box on the man's desk.

What could be in it? George could not resist.
He simply HAD to open it.

It was full of funny little pieces of all sorts of
shapes and all sorts of colors.

George took one out.
It looked like a
piece of candy.

Maybe it WAS candy. Maybe he could eat it. George put the piece in his mouth—and before he knew it, he had swallowed it.

A while later the man with the yellow hat came home. "Why, George," he said, "I see you have already opened the box with the jigsaw puzzle. It was supposed to be a surprise for you. Well, let's go to work on it."

Finally the puzzle was finished—
well, almost finished.
One piece was missing.

The man looked for it everywhere, but he could not find it. "That's strange," he said, "it's a brand-new puzzle. Well, it cannot be helped. Maybe we'll find it in the morning. Let's go to bed now, George."

The next morning George did not feel well. He had a tummy-ache and did not want to eat his breakfast.

The man was worried. He went to the telephone and called Doctor Baker. "I'll be over as soon as I can," said the doctor.

First Doctor Baker looked down George's throat and felt his tummy. Then he took out his stethoscope and listened. "I'm not sure what's wrong," he said. "You'd better take George to the hospital and have an X-ray taken. I'll call them and let them know you are coming."

"Don't worry, George," said the man when they were driving to the hospital, "you have been there before, when you broke your leg. Remember how nice the doctors and nurses were?"

George held his big rubber ball tight as they walked up the hospital steps.

A nurse took them down a long hallway to a room where she gave George something to drink that looked white and tasted sweet. "It is called barium," the nurse explained. "It helps the doctors find out what is wrong with you, George."

In the next room stood a big table, and a doctor was just putting on a heavy apron. Then he

gave the man one just like it. George was curious: Would he get one too? No, he did not.

"You get on that table, George," the doctor said. "I am going to take some X-ray pictures of your insides." He pushed a button and there was a funny noise. "There—now you may get up, and we will have the X-rays developed right away."

"Now let's see . . . There is something there that should not be," said the doctor when they were looking at the X-rays.

"Why, that looks like . . . I think that must be the piece that was missing in our jigsaw puzzle yesterday!" said the man. "Well, well, well," said the doctor, "at least we know now what is wrong with our little patient. I'll tell Doctor Baker right away. George will have to stay at the hospital for a few days. They'll put a tube down his throat to get the piece out. It's only a small operation. I'll call a nurse and have her take you to the admitting office."

Many people were waiting outside the office. George had to wait too.

"Look, Betsy," the woman next to him said to her little girl, "there is Curious George!" Betsy looked up for a moment, but she did not even smile. Betsy had never been to a hospital before. She was scared.

Finally it was George's turn.

A pretty young nurse took him to the next room
—my, how many rooms and how many nurses
there were! One nurse wrote down a lot of things
about George: his name and his address and what
was wrong with him. Another nurse put a bracelet
around his wrist. "It has
your name on it, George,"
she said, "so that every-
body knows who you are."

Then the pretty young nurse came back. "My name is Carol," she said. "I am going to take you to your room now—we call it the children's ward —and put you to bed. There will be lots of children to keep you company."

And so it was. There were a lot of children in the room. Some were up and around; others were in their beds, with a doctor or a nurse looking after them.

Dave was having a blood transfusion. Steve had his leg bandaged and was sitting in a go-cart. Betsy was in bed looking sad. George got the bed next to Betsy.

George was glad when he
was in his bed at last. His tummy
was hurting again.

The man sat with him for a while. "Now I have
to leave you, George," he finally said. "I'll be
back first thing in the morning before they take you
to the operating room.
Nurse Carol will tuck
you in when it's time
to sleep."

Then he left. George
just sat there and cried.

As he had promised, the man was back early next morning. The nurses were keeping George very busy. One nurse was taking his temperature; one was taking his blood pressure; one was giving him a pill ("To make you sleepy, George," she said), and one was getting ready to give him a shot.

"It's going to hurt, George," she said, "but only for a moment."

She took his arm, and George let out a scream.

"But the needle hasn't touched you yet," said the nurse, laughing. "There—now it's done. That wasn't so bad, was it?"

No, it really was not.

And anyway, it was over now.

By the time the attendant came with the stretcher to wheel him to the operating room, George was getting sleepy. He tried hard to stay awake. He was curious to see what would happen next.

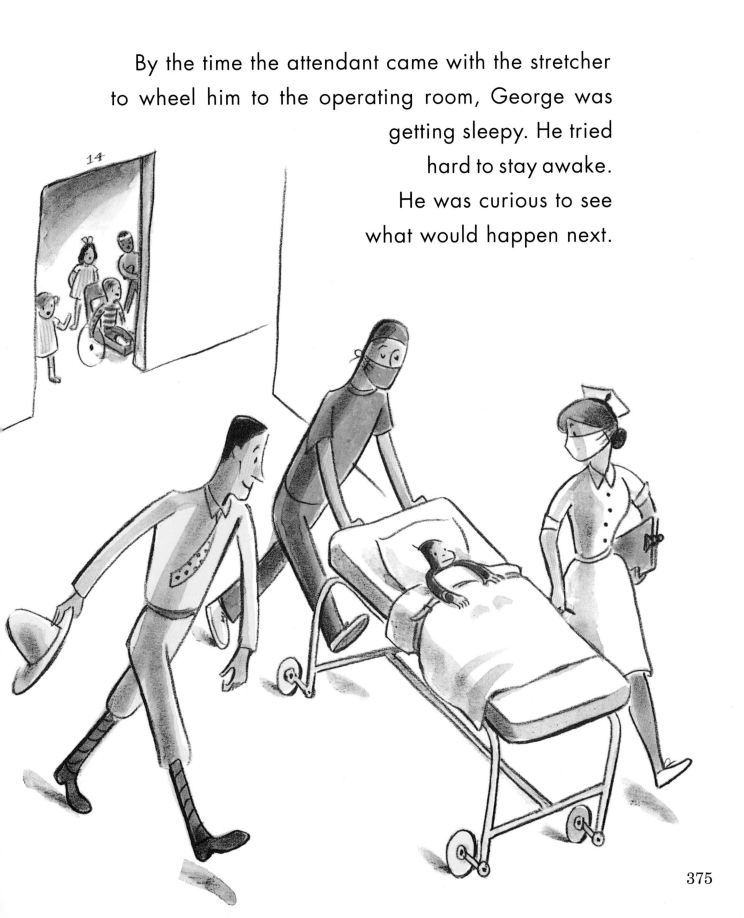

He could see a big table with bright lamps over it and doctors and nurses all around. They had caps on their heads and masks over their faces; only their eyes were showing.

One of the doctors winked at George and patted his head. It was Doctor Baker, who had

been to the house when it all had started. He looked funny with his mask on . . . And then George was fast asleep.

When George woke up he did not know what had happened. He did not even know where he was. Then he saw Nurse Carol. "It's all done, George," she said. "They got the piece out. In a day or two you will be running around again."

The man had brought him a picture book. But George felt sick and dizzy. His throat was hurting, too. He was not even curious about the new book. He closed his eyes again. "We'll let him sleep," said Nurse Carol. "The more he sleeps, the better."

The next morning George felt better. He even ate a dish of ice cream. Dr. Baker came to see him, and the man, of course, came too.

Betsy was watching him from time to time. She seemed a little less sad, but she still did not smile.

Steve wheeled his go-cart over to George's bed. "Tomorrow I can get up and try to walk," he said. "Boy, I can hardly wait."

"I'll take you to the playroom now, George," Nurse Carol said the next morning, "and in the afternoon your friend will come and take you home."

The playroom was full of children. A lady was showing Betsy how to use finger paint. There were all sorts of things to play with, even a puppet theater—and that was just the thing for George. He had four hands so could handle four puppets at the same time.

George gave
a real puppet show,
with a dragon
and a clown
and a bear
and a policeman.

The children laughed
and shouted,
and even Betsy
for the
first time
smiled a little.

There was a TV set in the playroom and also a
record player. George was curious: If he climbed
on the record player
and turned the switch,

would it go round
and round like a
real merry-go-round?

It did!
It started slowly,
then it went faster and
faster, and whoopee!
George had lost his
balance and was
sailing through the air . . .

383

Luckily George landed on a soft cushion. The children cheered, and Betsy smiled again. George was SO funny.

But then the play lady picked George up. "That's enough for now," she said. "You'd better take a nap before lunch. We have a big day ahead of us. The mayor is coming to visit the hospital today, and later on you will be going home, George."

When George woke up,
Steve was just taking his first steps.
A nurse was helping him, and the children were
watching.
    The go-cart was standing there empty.
George was curious.
He looked at it.
Then he climbed
into it.

Then he grabbed
the wheels and then, while
nobody was looking, he wheeled the go-cart right
out of the room.

George
could make
the go-cart go very fast.
This was fun! Down the hall he went.
By now the nurse had noticed that he
was gone and came running after him.
"George! George!" she shouted.

But George was
too excited to listen.
He wheeled around the corner
and down the ramp to the floor below,
where some men were busy pushing
lunch carts, and a lot of doctors and

nurses were showing the mayor around.

George tried to stop,
but it was too late.
WHAM!—the go-cart landed
right in the middle of everything.
Lunch carts tumbled. Spinach and scrambled
eggs and strawberry jam were all over the floor.
People fell over each other, and George was
thrown out of the go-cart and landed right in
the mayor's arms.

What a mess it was!

"You broke all my dishes!" someone cried.

"He ruined the go-cart!" complained another.

"What will the mayor think of it?" whispered someone else. And so it went.

Suddenly everybody looked up and listened. From above came happy laughter—and there stood Betsy, laughing, laughing, laughing. Then the children joined in, then the mayor started laughing, and finally everybody just laughed and laughed. Everybody, that is, except George.

Betsy came running down the ramp, threw her arms around George, and kissed him. "Don't be sad, George," she said. "The whole thing was SO funny! I never laughed so much in my life. I'm so glad you were in the hospital with me."

Now the director of the hospital spoke: "I am sorry this happened, Mr. Mayor," he said, "but I think we'll just clean up the mess and be done with it."

"George," he went on, "you've made a terrible mess. But you also made our sad little Betsy happy again, and that is more than any of us has done.

"And now I see your friend has just come to take you home. So, goodbye, George, and take good care of yourself."

The children
crowded around the
windows waving goodbye when
George and the man with the yellow
hat were finally leaving the hospital.

As the car was
turning into the driveway
Nurse Carol came running after them. "Here's
a little package with something that belongs to
you, George," she called. "But don't open it before you are home!"

George was curious—
well, who would not be?
The moment he reached home
he ripped the paper off,
tore open the box—
and THERE

was the piece
of the puzzle
that had caused
all the trouble!

"How nice of the doctor to save it for us!" said the man with the yellow hat. "And NOW we can finish the puzzle."

The End

Margret and H. A. Rey and their famous Curious George

by Louise Borden

Millions of us around the world have read one or more of the seven original Curious George stories included in this seventy-fifth anniversary edition. My favorites growing up were *Curious George Takes a Job* and *Curious George Rides a Bike.*

Years after reading those yellow books, I found out what the H and the A stand for in H. A. Rey . . . and that echoes of H.A.'s life, and those of his wife, Margret, appear in the illustrations of their stories. Maybe you can discover them too.

Early Years

Hans Augusto Reyersbach was born in Hamburg, Germany, close to the North Sea. As a boy, he watched the ships of the world sail into port and unload their cargoes on the docks of the river Elbe.

H.A. didn't know then he would grow up to live on three continents . . . and be known for creating the most famous monkey in the world.

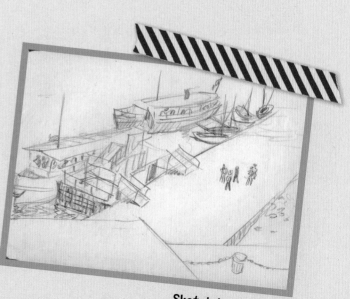

Sketch by H. A. Rey.

Hans had one brother and two sisters. From an early age he showed a talent for drawing horses and all kinds of things. And he could mimic the roars of the lions he saw in the Hagenbeck Zoo, not far from his house.

When Hans turned ten on September 16, 1908, Margarete Elisabeth Waldstein was only two years old. Her parents lived near the Reyersbachs. Both families were Jewish, and were friends.

In 1914, Germany went to war against England, France, and Russia.

Margarete Waldstein was now eight years old, and had two sisters and two brothers.

Hans Reyersbach was in high school and a student of languages. But he still loved to draw. After graduation, Hans was drafted into the German army to serve as a soldier.

Hans with his unit.

At the front, he carried a pocket guide of the stars. "Hmm," Hans told himself on clear nights. "This star guide is not easy to understand . . ." never guessing he would later create two star guides of his own.

404

When Germany lost the war in 1918, Hans went home to Hamburg. To help pay for college classes, he painted circus posters . . . and met clowns and acrobats as he sketched the big ring.

Original sketch from *Curious George Rides a Bike.*

Then, in the early 1920s at a party at the Waldstein home, Hans saw Margarete for the first time . . . when she slid down a banister. Already, Margarete, with her smile and her curls, had the sparkle and confidence she would carry the rest of her life.

Brazil

S.S. Albert Ballin.

Times were hard after the war, so Hans joined a relative's import-export business. He left Germany in 1925, sailing from Hamburg to New York City aboard the *Albert Ballin*. Six months later, H.A. went on to Rio de Janeiro, Brazil. There he learned Portuguese and traveled to the Amazon River. Ten years went by.

In Hamburg, Margarete Waldstein was now grown up. She studied art at the famous Bauhaus, and then in Düsseldorf. Margarete also had a love for photography.

Seal from Margarete's school certificate.

Margarete and her siblings.

When Adolf Hitler became the leader of Germany in 1933, his Nazi laws changed life for German Jews.

Margarete moved to London, England, to work as a photographer. Her parents and family would also leave Hamburg because of Hitler's anti-Jewish laws. In 1935, Margarete bought a ticket to sail to Brazil, and packed her camera. She knew Hans Reyersbach, her family friend, was there.

Map of Brazil illustrated by Hans.

Photo taken by Margarete.

The two artists from Hamburg shared ideas and began to work together. Margarete changed her first name to Margret and Hans shortened his last name to Rey.

H.A. and Margret made a great team. They soon married and started the first husband-and-wife advertising agency in Rio.

In 1936, carrying new Brazilian passports, the Reys sailed back to Europe for a belated honeymoon.

France

During their travels, they went to Paris. Instead of visiting for a few weeks, Margret and Hans stayed for four years.

The Reys lived here—at the Terrass Hotel.

Soon the Reys began to create books and found publishers in Paris and London. Hans was the thinker with vision. Margret was the art director and organizer.

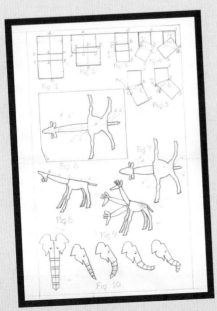

H.A.'s first books in Paris were wordless, and for grownups. Hans also designed paper punch-outs.

And . . . he loved to draw giraffes. His first book for children was about a giraffe and nine monkeys without tails.

Rafi et les 9 Singes was published in France in 1939 and also in England, as *Raffy and the Nine Monkeys*.

On September 1, 1939, the shadow of war covered Europe once again. That day, Adolf Hitler sent his soldiers into Poland. France and England soon declared war on Germany.

Margret and Hans left Paris and traveled south to Château Feuga, an old castle owned by German friends. There, Hans worked on a new book starring Fifi, the youngest monkey in the Raffy book. Fifi was a curious monkey who had a friend, the man with the yellow hat (who looked like a fellow the Reys had both known in Hamburg).

Château Feuga.

409

H.A. also painted pictures for a book about a penguin named Whiteblack. Margret worked on the design and typed the words. "Travelers always have lots of stories . . ." And the Reys were pleased with their new lift-the-flap book.

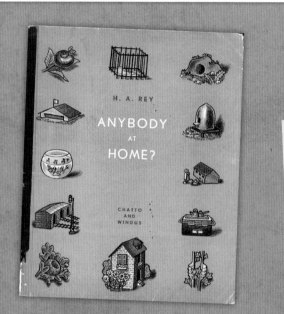

On Christmas Eve, they returned to their apartment at the Terrass Hotel.
Then in April 1940, the two artists went to a town in Normandy to work near the sea.

Hans' advance receipt.

Their French publisher, Gallimard, sent Hans a contract, and advance money, for *The Adventures of Fifi* and two other books.

And the war? On May 10, 1940, Hitler's troops invaded France.

Margret and H.A. hurried back to Paris and made a plan to go to America, where Margret's sister Mary was living. As German tanks rattled closer to the capital, there was bedlam on the streets of Paris. People fled from the city by car, horse, bicycle, and foot.

The Reys took their winter coats and their manuscripts and fled Paris on bicycles that Hans had assembled himself.

H.A. and Margret traveled to Portugal, then Brazil, and finally docked in New York City on October 14, 1940. As Hans said: "One never forgets the day you arrive in America . . ."

New York City

On October 17, H.A. sent a postcard to Grace Hogarth, one of their London editors, who was now at Houghton Mifflin in Boston.

In November, Mrs. Hogarth came to New York and offered Hans a contract for four of the manuscripts the Reys had carried from Paris, including *The Adventures of Fifi*. She asked that Fifi's name be changed to a stronger, more American name. Hmm . . . maybe . . . George? *Curious George* was published on August 17, 1941.

In New York City, Margret and H.A. lived on Perry Street and on West 236th Street until they moved to 42 Washington Square.

Design by H.A. Rey.

"I never go above 14th Street . . . everything I need is here," Hans said of their life in Greenwich Village.

The Reys loved the energy in New York City. They always had a cocker spaniel for company: first Charcoal (Charky), followed by Jamie, Scoopy, Andy, and finally, in 1993, Jeannie.

Sometimes Margret wrote her own stories. Hans also illustrated books by other writers.

Illustration from *The Park Book* dummy.

In 1946, their Curious George readers had asked for a new book. Hmm . . .

A Fifth Avenue scene, a building with windows to wash, a subway, a newsstand, a movie . . . (and, of course, the man with the yellow hat) became parts of *Curious George Takes a Job*, published in 1947. The text seems simple, but it took the Reys more than a year to find just the right trouble for George to get into . . . and to get out of.

Look for Margret strolling with her dog. Look for Hans with his sketchbook next to his pal Mr. Jackson.

See Charky at the newsstand and the movie?

Is that H.A. in 14C?

In 1949, Margret and H.A. moved to 82 Washington Place. Hans rented a room nearby for his studio.

Sketch of Washington Place apartment.

H.A. in his studio.

"The coming of an idea is wonderful and exciting . . . the making of the first sketches is fun too since I love drawing . . . I do not mean to say you feel happy every minute . . . There are times when you run into snags." (H.A.)

H.A. liked to give little stories to many of the extra characters in his books.

Follow the story of the kitten in *Curious George Takes a Job*. And look for the mini-story about the mice or the balloon man in *Curious George*.

The third Curious George book, *Curious George Rides a Bike,* was published in 1952 . . . with a bicycle and a newsboy, a neighborhood, a river, a fleet of paper boats, a traveling circus, and a lost little bear.

Look for Charky and Margret in the neighborhood.

Find the Reys and Charky at the show.

Look at the blue car's license plate. What do you think "CG3" stands for?

The Reys continued to love their Greenwich Village neighborhood. Margret once said, "Every night we had a dog meeting on the square. Fifteen or twenty dogs from the neighborhood played together. We had a silent agreement with the police to let our dogs off the leash at night."

During this happy time, the fourth Curious George book was created. *Curious George Gets a Medal,* published in 1957, has a comic adventure with soapsuds and a hose. (This actually happened to an aspiring chemist the Reys had known years before in Hamburg.) George causes an uproar and redeems himself by taking a ride on a rocket.

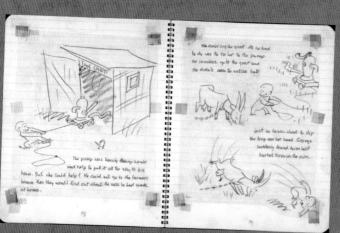

Original sketch from *Curious George Gets a Medal.*

When real monkeys were later sent into outer space, Margret liked to joke that George was their inspiration.

See the blue truck with "CG4"? And the Reys' dog Jamie on the last page?

Hans and Margret working together.

In the late 1950s, educators were abuzz about the best way to teach beginning readers: short lines with simple vocabulary. So Margret typed a list of 219 words. What should the book be about?

"Hmm," said Hans. "I like kites . . . "
The Reys took Jamie for a stroll and plotted scenes for a good story.
"Would George do this?"
"No, George would do that."
Gradually the story took shape.

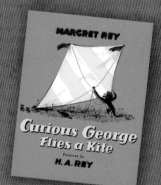

Dummy spread from *Curious George Flies a Kite*.

Original sketch from *Curious George Flies a Kite*.

In 1958, *Curious George Flies a Kite* appeared in bookstores and libraries. Margret hoped kids wouldn't notice the new easy-to-read style. Hans hoped kids would notice the little robin and "CG5."

Cambridge

On to another adventure, the Reys left New York City in 1963 and moved to Cambridge, Massachusetts. Hilliard Street, number 12, and then 14, became their home.

The creators of George were now popular speakers at book events. A few times, Hans even roared like a lion.

Soon, *Curious George Learns the Alphabet* brought letters and words to readers in a classic and clever Rey way. H.A. said: "This book was all mine."

Dummy spread from *Curious George Learns the Alphabet.*

Original sketch from *Curious George Learns the Alphabet.*

In 1966, *Curious George Goes to the Hospital* was published after Children's Hospital in Boston asked the Reys to create a book to ease the fear of a first visit for kids.

Setting the story in just one place was a challenge for Margret and Hans. A jigsaw puzzle piece and George's curiosity lead to a tummyache and surgery.

Can you find Margret and Scoopy by the curb?

"This book gave us the most satisfaction of all," Margret said, after hundreds of parents wrote thank-you letters to the Reys.

Nancy Gieschen
117 Pierce St
Manassas Park, Va.
10/29/75
22110

Dear Mr. Rey,

Thank you! Because of your book Curious George goes to the Hospital, my daughter Erika eats spinach, scrambled eggs, & strawberry jam. She also gave up her crib and likes her youth bed because C.G. sleeps in a bed.

Thank You!
Nancy Gieschen

These seven tales about George and his antics have been translated into sixteen different languages.

George's curiosity is now famous around the globe. H.A., who once said in an interview, "We're in the monkey business, you might say . . ." died a few weeks before his seventy-ninth birthday.

Margret lived into her ninety-first year at 14 Hilliard Street, walking with her dog Jeannie and their friend Lay Lee Ong to Harvard Square . . . and sharing her beloved George with the children of the world.

A selection of New Year's cards designed by H.A.

In 1944, Hans wrote on an annual New Year's card: "Let's think of the future: that's where we shall spend the rest of our lives."

Remember Hans Augusto Reyersbach, the boy who spent hours at the zoo in Hamburg? Remember Margarete Elisabeth Waldstein, who slid down the banister of her house?

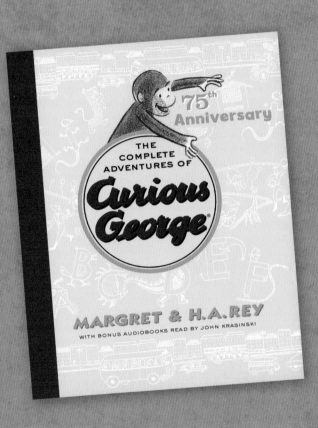

How lucky we are, generations of readers, to have the books of these two artists to carry ahead in our twenty-first century.

Someday, if you travel beyond our planet Earth, the courage of a little monkey will be in your pocket . . . because Curious George, born on pages in wartime France, has been there before you, showing you the way.

This book's end papers is a map of the World of Curious George, created by the illustrator Anna Grossnickle Hines in celebration of the 75th anniversary of Curious George. As you explore the map you will find the locations of all of George's adventures . . . the dock where he tried to catch a fish, the launch where he flew into space, the skyscraper in need of a window washer, the hospital he visited to remove a swallowed puzzle piece, and so much more!

TAKE A CLOSER LOOK AT THE END PAPERS
AND SEE IF YOU CAN FIND . . .

- the subway entrance
- the phone booth
- the newspaper stand
- the balloon man
- the bunny house
  (and a couple of bunnies)

- newspaper boats
- a kite (hint: it's stuck in a tree)
- the man with the yellow hat (and George)
- George's friend Bill
- Margret Rey
- H. A. Rey

HANS AUGUSTO REY (1898–1977) met his wife-to-be, **MARGRET REY** (1906–1996), at a party in her father's home in Germany. When he first caught a glimpse of her, she was sliding down the banister. They lived in Rio de Janeiro and Paris before moving to New York City and eventually settling in Cambridge, Massachusetts. Throughout their lives the Reys created many lively picture books together, but it is their incorrigible little monkey, Curious George, who has become an American icon, selling millions of books and capturing the hearts of readers everywhere.

LOUISE BORDEN is the author of thirty books for young readers, both fiction and nonfiction, including *The Journey That Saved Curious George,* illustrated by Allan Drummond, and *His Name Was Raoul Wallenberg.* Her subjects range from kindergarten to baseball to World War II. Louise and her husband, Peter, have three grown children and live in Cincinnati, Ohio.

JOHN KRASINSKI has established himself as one of the most exciting talents as an actor, writer, and director, engaging audiences on the big and small screen. Krasinski notably starred on NBC's Emmy®–winning smash hit *The Office* for nine seasons, where he portrayed the charming boy-next-door Jim Halpert. Born and raised in Newton, Massachusetts, Krasinski currently resides in Los Angeles with his wife, Emily Blunt, and their family.

IMAGE CREDITS

[1] H.A. & Margret Rey Papers, de Grummond Children's Literature Collection, The University of Southern Mississippi

[2] Houghton Mifflin Harcourt Publishing Company

[3] akg-images

[4] www.moore-mccormack.com

[5] National Archives/Ancestry.com

[6] From the collection of Louise Borden

[7] From the collection of Lay Lee Ong

[8] © Frazer Harrison/Getty Images

Pages **401**: book illustrations [2], photos [1]; **402**: photo [1], boat watercolor [1], pencil sketch [1]; **403**: watercolor [1], photo [1], book illustrations [2]; **404**: photos [1], covers [2]; **405**: sketch [1], photo [1], cover [2]; **406**: family photo [1], school seal [1], camera photo [3], ship [5]; **407**: map [1], photo [1], book illustration [1], invite [7]; **408**: pencil sketch [1], photo [6], cover [6], book illustration [6]; **409**: French cover [1], English cover [2], book illustrations [2], color photo [1], black-and-white photo [3]; **410**: photo [1], receipt [1], covers [2], book illustration [2]; **411**: black-and-white photos [3], Statue of Liberty [3], ship [4]; **412**: Fifi [1], sketch [1], CG with phone [2], covers [2]; **413**: Self-portrait [1], photos [1], spread [1], book illustration [2]; **414**: cover [2], illustrations [2], photo [3]; **415**: pencil sketch [1], photo [1], book illustrations [2]; **416**: cover and book illustrations [2]; **417**: photo [1], illustrations [2]; **418**: pencil sketch [1], cover and book illustrations [2]; **419**: photos [1], pencil sketch [1], spread [1], cover [2], book illustrations [2]; **420**: black-and-white photo [1], pencil sketch [1], spread [1], cover [2], illustration [2], color photo [6]; **421**: pencil sketch [1], letter [1], covers and illustrations [2]; **422**: photos and cards [1]; **423**: photo [1], cover and illustration [2]; **427**: John Krasinski photo [8].